# Lemuel the Fool

This one is for Karen, who can always spot a fool.

—M. U.

For my daughter, Anna.

—S. L.

Ω

Published by
PEACHTREE PUBLISHING COMPANY INC.
1700 Chattahoochee Avenue
Atlanta, Georgia 30318-2112
*www.peachtree-online.com*

Text © 2001 by Myron Uhlberg
Illustrations © 2001 by Sonja Lamut

First trade paperback edition published in 2021

Printed and manufactured in October 2020 by Toppan Leefung in China

Book design by Sonja Lamut and Loraine M. Joyner
Book composition by Melanie McMahon Ives

This book is smythe-sewn; the body of the text is set in 15pt Belwe on 130 gsm matte art paper.

10 9 8 7 6 5 4 3 2 1 (hardcover)
10 9 8 7 6 5 4 3 2 1 (trade paperback)

HC ISBN: 978-1-56145-220-0
PB ISBN: 978-1-68263-314-4

CIP Code: 052031.8K1/B1654/A7

# Lemuel the Fool

Myron Uhlberg

Illustrated by
Sonja Lamut

PEACHTREE
ATLANTA

Once there was a man named Lemuel.
He lived in a small fishing village by the sea.

At night, while the other villagers dreamed of catching fish, big fish, Lemuel dreamed of sailing over the horizon to see the wonderful city there surely must be on the other side of the water.

Every morning, as the stars began to fade in the night sky, Lemuel and the other villagers set out in their little boats to catch fish. They sailed toward the horizon, and as the sky turned pink and the sun rose, they cast their nets into the water.

The villagers fished and imagined a rich, finny harvest. Lemuel dreamed and imagined an enchanted, magical city.

Lemuel was possessed. His dream grew stronger. The magical city by the edge of the sea just over the horizon was all he thought about, day in and day out.

His wife became annoyed, and his son soon tired of hearing of his father's dream. The villagers thought him a fool.

One day, Lemuel announced to his wife, "Essie, on this very day, I will begin to build a boat that will take me over the horizon. I must see the city that lies on the other side of the water."

"But how will Sol and I live when you are gone on your foolish voyage?" said Essie in despair.

"I will stay out at sea an hour extra every day," Lemuel replied. "And the fish that I catch in that time I will salt and store for the two of you until I return."

"Aren't we enough for you to be happy?" Essie asked.

"You and Sol are my treasure and my light," Lemuel answered. "But I must see the enchanted city before I die."

Every night, when the moon rode high in the sky, Lemuel worked on his boat. And every morning when the moon was low and the stars began to fade, Lemuel set out with the other villagers to catch fish.

Finally the boat was ready.

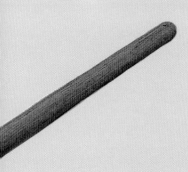

"I leave tomorrow on the morning tide," Lemuel announced to Essie.

"Fool!" she said. "With me and your son, in our village, you have been happy. But for you that is not enough. So go."

Lemuel had built well. The tall sails quickly filled, and the boat was soon leaping from wave to wave, pointed straight at the horizon.

Lemuel had tied a red scarf on the bow of his boat and attached to the stern a long line that trailed in the water behind. He reasoned that as long as he followed the red scarf, which was in front of him, and stayed ahead of the rope, which trailed behind, he would be sailing in the right direction.

No sooner had Lemuel sailed out of sight of land than a great storm arose.

The sky darkened as day turned into night. The howling winds blew in every direction, shouldering Lemuel's boat, driving it up and down waves as high as mountains.

Lemuel was swept off his feet. Striking his head on the mast, he lost consciousness.

When, after a time, he came to his senses, the storm had passed, and the boat was gently rocking aimlessly on the now-calm sea.

"How fortunate I am to have survived the storm," thought Lemuel.

Resetting the sails, Lemuel aimed his boat in the direction of the red scarf, while carefully observing that the rope did, indeed, trail behind.

"How clever I am," he said, "to have had the foresight to use the scarf to point me in the right direction."

After sailing a surprisingly short while, Lemuel sighted land. "At last!" he exclaimed. "I have found the enchanted village." He could hardly contain his excitement.

As his boat drew closer to the shore, he observed fishing boats drawn up onto the beach, their sails furled, their anchors set in the sand.

"How curious," he thought. "These boats look very much like the boats that we use back home to fish. If I didn't know better, I'd think that red one with the yellow sail was Hershel's boat."

ailing right onto the beach, as he did back home, Lemuel dropped the sails, set the anchor in the sand, and eagerly set out to explore this fine new place.

He was surprised to see a crowd of men standing impatiently in line, waiting to unload their catch onto a big scale.

"How strange," he thought. "The fishermen in this place follow the same procedures as we do back home. And look, they push and shove and argue just as we do. I suppose people are the same the world over."

So intent was Lemuel on the sight of the fishermen that he failed to see the cats milling about his legs. Their hissing and spitting at each other finally caught his attention.

"My goodness," he thought. "The cats here act just like the cats back home. They even look the same, especially the orange one with the short tail and the missing ear. Cats must look the same the world over."

Walking away from the beach, he began to explore this new town, surprisingly so like his own.

Wandering up and down familiar narrow streets filled with familiar-looking people and lined with simple, familiar houses, he was at first disappointed, then shocked.

"This looks exactly like my village back home," he said to himself in amazement. "Do all the villages the world over look the same?"

As he rounded the corner at the head of a strangely familiar crooked street, he stopped dead in his tracks. His jaw dropped in amazement. "Am I dreaming?" he said. "This looks like my street. And that house looks like my house. And, my goodness, the boy sitting on the steps looks like my son, Sollie."

Just then, a woman came out the front door. "Lemuel," she said. "What are you doing home so early?"

Now, Lemuel was at a loss for words. This woman was the precise twin of his own wife, Essie, and somehow she knew his name.

"Just as well," the woman said. "Close your mouth. Come in at once. Clean up. Change your clothes. Hurry. Dinner's on the table."

"Why, this woman is just as bossy as my dear Essie!" Lemuel said.

Once inside the house, Lemuel truly believed he had lost his mind. There, the same pine table and chairs as the ones in his house. Hanging from the windows, the same white curtains. On the floor, the same worn rug.

"Don't just stand there!" the woman who looked like Essie said. "Your dinner's growing cold."

After washing off the smell of the sea and changing into clothes that fit him perfectly, Lemuel sat down at the table.

"Who are you people?" he asked the woman and the boy. "And how do you know my name?"

"What a foolish question," the woman answered. "You're Lemuel, my husband. And you know very well that I am Essie, your wife. And this is Sol, your son."

"I know no such thing," Lemuel announced. "You could not possibly be my wife. And this is surely not my son. They are back home waiting for me. Although, I must admit, you do resemble them."

"Oh, my dear husband, you are surely a fool. But even fools get hungry. So eat!"

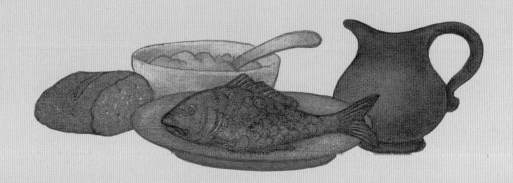

Late that night, when the woman who looked like his wife and the boy who looked like his son were asleep, Lemuel changed back into his own clothes and quietly crept from the house.

"I've had enough of this madness," he thought. "I will sail home immediately."

The strange town that looked so like his own was silent as he shoved his boat back into the water and set sail toward the horizon for home.

No sooner had he lost sight of land than Lemuel, confused beyond understanding, fell into a deep sleep.

The rays of the rising sun falling across his face
woke him with a start.

With the horizon in front of him, Lemuel aimed his
boat in the direction of the red scarf, while carefully
observing that the rope did, indeed, trail behind.

In a surprisingly short time, he sighted land. He quickly recognized the beach of his town. With joy in his heart, he sailed up onto the familiar beach, dropped the sails, and set the anchor in the sand.

"There is Hershel's boat," he said, looking at the red boat with the yellow sail. "I'd know it anywhere."

Rushing into the village, he could hardly contain his
excitement at being home again.

"Won't Essie and Sollie be happy to see me," he thought.
"I'm sure they missed me."

Bursting through the door of his house, he shouted,
"I'm home! I'm home!"

"Of course you're home, you fool," Essie said. "Where else in the world could you possibly be?"